VERSES FOR FLEUR

country holds all stories
even the broken ones
especially the broken ones

HEATHER ANNE GORDON

This print edition published in 2025
by Centred in Choice

Title: Verses for Fleur

Author: © Heather Anne Gordon
verses written 2020 - 2024

First published by Centred in Choice
ABN 17 601 690 975

A catalogue record for this book is available from the National Library of Australia

ISBN 978-1-7635635-7-5

Author: © Heather Anne Gordon
Title: Verses for Fleur

Acknowledgement:
We acknowledge and respect the deep spiritual connection and the relationship that First Nations people have to Country.
Country takes in everything within the landscape – landforms, waters, air, trees, rocks, plants, animals, foods, medicines, minerals, stories, and special places.
Connections to Country include cultural practices, knowledge, songs, stories, and art, as well as all people: past, present, and future.

Cover Design: Karren Marree Engel
original photographs by Heather

Internal Design: Karen Marree Engel

First Reader: Deb Selway

Dedicated to: VWB (1946 – 2024)

Published by Centred in Choice
Sharing Australian voices, stories, strategies, and skills with the world.
https://centredinchoice.com
PO Box 448 Alice Springs Northern Territory
0871 Australia

being

heather anne gordon is a south australian writer whose words
grow from country itself
shaped by decades of journals
and a deep respect
for first nations knowledge
and ways of living
her verses explore how people
connect to land
to each other
to renewal
inspired by those who walk gently
and live sustainably
her stories flow like rivers through soil
and being
carrying care
community
longing
and belonging

caring for country is not a task
it is a listening
a leaning in to breath and bark
to creek and wind and stone
it is knowing the pulse beneath our feet
the memory carried by seed and sand
it is the work of hands and heart together
guided by those who came before
who mapped the stars and seasons
in story and in silence
we walk their lines with respect
we tend the soil with humility
for country is not owned
it is held
for a moment
and then passed on
to those who will
listen again

Contents

healing

under the marltarra
two women meet again
among vines and dust
one from the soil
one from far away
grief carried in her breath
love returns like water
through roots
healing through country
through kind hands
through the calm
a shetland sheep dog called cloud
and the quiet knowing
that tending
is another name for love

the sun slants low
across the southern valley
gold light
spilling through the lush green vines
claire lifts her face to it
the day's work pressed into her skin
she wipes her brow with a handkerchief
stiff with dried sweat and dust
shakes loose the honey brown curls
feels the faintest breeze
touch the back of her neck
beneath the canopy
cloud the dog waits
a soft grey shape in the green
ears flicking blue eyes steady
faithful as shadow

claire murmurs to her
good girl cloud waiting in this heat
where do you think
that brother of mine has gone
he promised seven o'clock
and the day is nearly done
i am nearly done

kangaroos have torn the drip line again
the black tubing coiled and stubborn
claire bends and pulls and mends
her fingers know the work
her mind drifts to water and stillness
to some imagined place where the air is cool
where she floats and forgets the vines

cloud listens in silence
but her head turns sharply
and claire's breath catches
for a heartbeat she thinks *snake*
then hears the slow hum of diesel
the sound of her brother's ute
rolling up the end of the row

thank goodness cloud
we are saved
no more of this toil today

claire gathers cloud's water bowl
tips the last of the contents
on to the waiting earth
they walk side by side through the row
the air heavy with ripening
baumé and promise

a voice carries on the wind
sorry i am late claire
look who i found at the meeting

claire shields her eyes against the light
and sees a tall figure beside the ute
willowy and framed by sky
a flash of white teeth and laughter
then another voice
familiar and distant as memory
and the air around them seems to still

bonsoir mademoiselle claire
the words fall bright across the vines
claire's heart stumbles
the voice too familiar
too dangerous in the slow warm air

fleur laurent
fabulous fleur
the french food and wine writer
who once turned the valley inside out
with her laughter
her questions
her generous smile
fleur had followed claire
everywhere
that vintage
asking about soil
pruning
weather
under the pretext of writing
but her eyes told another story

claire remembers that night
the last before fleur fled the valley
the soft rain
the scent of crushed grapes
the sudden hunger between them
now almost three years gone
still the memory burns

claire feels the heat rise under her skin
tries to tame it with reason
three years of silence
claire tells herself
it means nothing
it must mean nothing

yet as she strides toward the ute
the air thickens
her shirt clings with leaf dust and sweat
jeans marked by earth
her hair a tangle of sun and fatigue
still she lifts her chin

fleur stands radiant
the light catching her dark hair
a spark in her eyes
that claire cannot meet
for long

fleur
what a surprise
when did you arrive
where are you staying

the words come steadily
but inside
her pulse throbs
wildly

the light of the valley strikes her
like memory
warm and merciless blue after years of grey sky
fleur blinks against it
the air alive with birds and dust
the colour of vines so green
it almost hurts

fleur laurent
she whispers her own name
as if to anchor herself
the woman who once wrote
of pleasure and place
now feels the weight of loss
in every breath
her mother gone
to the first wave of covid sickness
her father faded
slowly
in its long cruel shadow
until there is no one left
to call her home

so she has come here
to the only place that always felt kind
marltarra with its rolling hills
and one woman she never forgot

but how to speak after silence
how to smile when her heart still trembles
she paints the brightness on her face
she laughs at mike's jokes
she lets her eyes wander to claire
moving among the vines
strong and sure and sunlit
her shirt streaked with leaf dust and sweat
a scientist
a woman of the soil
and fleur's throat tightens

she remembers that night
the taste of crushed grapes
the breathless laughter
the wild believing that the world
could not end

bonsoir madamoiselle claire she had called
too light
too careless
possibly mocking
but it was the only way to hide
the quake inside

and now as claire steps closer
fleur feels her chest fill with ache
the scent of earth and eucalyptus
something unnamed
she wonders if love can bloom again
in earth so scorched by lockdowns and loss

claire feels it before it happens
fleur's hand reaching slow and sure
the air between them shimmering
she thrusts her own hand forward fast
turns a greeting into distance
but the moment their palms meet
a current leaps skin to heart
oh no claire thinks
not again

fleur smiles
all sunlight and charm
her shadow falling across claire's face
bareheaded radiant full of scent and summer
claire's resolve melts
her grin escapes uninvited
blue eyes bright as sky after rain

claire how lovely to see you
enchanté

the sound of the word
a caress
fleur leans in arms wide
and before claire can retreat
she is wrapped in warmth and musk
the memory of that one night
flares alive beneath her ribs
her heart stumbling in her chest
this cannot be happening she thinks
not here not now not like this

then the smell of sweat and soil returns
claire pulls free laughing too loudly
oh fleur
i have been working all day
i am filthy and probably smell like compost
i apologise for the state of me

claire turns to her brother
uses his presence like a shield
where have you been mike
cloud and i are ready to melt

cloud wags her tail as if to agree
fleur only smiles
and the space between them hums
with everything
not yet said

the ute smells of dust and diesel
mike at the wheel talking nonstop
his words tumbling like small stones
down a hill
about the meeting
the funding
the new irrigation trial
and how good it is
that fleur has come back
how she will love seeing
what they have done at marltarra
how the valley has changed
since her last vintage here

claire nods at the right times
her eyes fixed on the window
the vines blurring green and bright
her pulse still unsteady from that touch
cloud crouched quietly in the footwell
claire can feel fleur
on the bench seat beside her
close enough
that the air between them feels charged
like the moment before thunder breaks

fleur listens to mike with polite smiles
her hands folded tight in her lap
she lets his words wash over her
grateful for his enthusiasm
afraid of what silence would reveal

claire glances once
catches the line of fleur's jaw
the weariness there under the brightness
and her chest tightens
with an ache
she does not want to name

mike keeps talking
about soil health
about resilience
about the next festival
and how the valley needs good stories again
claire forces a smile
says something about the vines holding up
but her mind drifts
to the night she cannot forget
to the warmth still ghosting her skin

as they turn into the drive at marltarra
the late sun glows through the gums
their long shadows
stretching across the paddock
cloud lifts her head from the footwell
yawns once
home

mike brakes
grinning
we will open a bottle to celebrate
he says
claire is already stepping down
the air cool on her face
her heart far too warm

chapter six the homestead

the homestead glows in the folding light
windows lit with gold and kitchen laughter
sue already at the bench
apron tied
hair loose
calling out as they walk in
welcome home workers
and *welcome back to the valley fleur*

mike drops his hat on the hook
starts uncorking a bottle
before his boots are off
talking all at once
about vines and visitors
the possible rain coming
his words filling the room like music

fleur stands just inside the doorway
the smell of garlic bread and eucalyptus
catching her breath
fleur feels the ache
of wanting to belong
something she has not felt for a long time
she runs her hand through her hair
smiles when cloud noses her knee

claire busies herself with glasses and plates
her face half hidden in the cupboard's shadow
but her voice softens
it's good to have company again
and her brother nods grinning
as if it were the most delightful thing in the world

they sit outside to eat
the table wide with light and colour
cheese olives grilled vegetables
a salad cut fresh from the garden
mike raises his glass to friends old and new
to good soil and strong hearts
and the wine glows amber
in the fading sun

fleur tastes it
feels the warmth bloom through her
the first true ease in months
she looks at claire across the table
and catches her gaze
only for a heartbeat
but long enough to feel the old spark stir

the night deepens
frogs begin their chorus down by the dam
and cloud curls beneath the table
content in the hum of voices

fleur listens to the crickets
the rustle of leaves
to the hum of words
unsaid beneath the talk
the ones that belong only to claire and her

the house drifts into quiet
mike and sue's chat fading behind the door
the scent of grilled vegetables and wine
lingering in the air
cloud pads softly beside claire
her paws a whisper
on the old verandah boards

outside the sky is wide and velvet
stars spill like dust across the dark
somewhere an owl calls
and the vines breathe
in the cool of night

claire leans on the railing
lets the day fall away
the work
the heat
the memory of fleur's touch
until she hears
the faint creak of a chair
and sees her there

fleur sits in the half light
wrapped in a shawl too thin for the chill
barefoot
legs folded beneath her
a glass of water
glinting in her hand
her face turned upward
as if listening for ghosts

claire hesitates
then steps closer
you can't sleep either
her voice low so as not to wake
the house

fleur smiles
tired and lovely
sleep and i are no longer friends
the night has too many stories to tell

they wait there a moment
the air between them filled
with everything they cannot yet name
then claire lowers herself into the chair
beside fleur
the silence becomes
companionable

cloud curls at their feet
sighing
somewhere a fox screams from the ridge
the stars seem to lean closer
as if curious

fleur speaks softly of alsace
of long months of sirens
closed windows
temporary field hospitals
the surge of infections
the impact on health workers
the taste of fear

the strange peace
that follows grief
claire listens
her heart opening
like soil after rain

and when their eyes meet
there is no need for words
only knowing
that something once lost
is found again
under the southern cross

the morning drifts in
on pale mist
soft as breath across the paddocks
dew shines on blades of grass
cloud awake
her coat ghosting through the vineyard
chasing the rowdy galahs
from their breakfast
their wings flashing rose and grey
against the light

claire stands on the verandah
hands wrapped around a ceramic mug
the first coffee of the day
steam curling
like thought in the chill air
the valley below still half asleep
only the magpies singing the sun awake

fleur steps out barefoot
hair tousled
her cardigan borrowed from a chair
she murmurs
good morning in her low french voice
the sound settles into claire's chest
like warmth
they stand side by side
the silence between them gentle
not strained
watching the fog lift from the vines

fleur sighs
this place breathes she says
in alsace the air felt thin
here it feels alive
fleur looks out across marltarra
and claire nods and murmurs
the air and soil heal if you let it
it just takes time and care

fleur glances at her
you speak of soil as if it were a person
claire smiles
maybe it is
every handful
full of stories and scars
just like us

they sip their coffee
the mist slowly opens
revealing rows of green
the glint of water
somewhere mike's ute starts
in the distance
the spell breaks
but softly
like waking
from a dream you wish would linger

cloud bounds back up the hill
wriggles in excitement to see them
both women laugh
the sound light and clean
carried on the morning air

chapter nine the line of water

the sun is soft still climbing
light gold and kind across the vines
the ground cool underfoot
kangaroo prints pressed deep in the damp
a trail of mischief through the rows

claire crouches
to finish the job she began the day before
the black tubing slick with dew
her fingers steady and sure
threading the drip line through wire and clip
tightening the join until water hums again
a pulse beneath the earth

fleur watches
her breath slow with the rhythm of claire's work
the quiet competence
the care
the way she touches the land
like an old friend
there is beauty in this fleur thinks
not the beauty of cities or wine glasses
but of hands that mend what others forget

cloud trots behind them
a little grey blur at claire's feet
ears flicking
tail wagging
sniffing each post as if counting their progress
faithful shadow in the morning light

claire stands wiping her hands on her jeans
there we go claire says
one less leak in the system
fleur smiles
you make it sound easy
it's not easy claire answers
but it's worth it

they walk slowly through the vines
rows stretching neat and green
the air thick with the scent of promise
somewhere between talk and silence
their shoulders brush once
not accident but not confession
just the gentle meeting
of two lives mending

cloud darts ahead
chasing the shimmer of light through leaves
the drip line sings softly behind them
and the valley breathes

chapter ten under the marltarra gums

they stop where the trees gather
their trunks grey and peeling
the ground cool and dappled
the air sweet with balm and earth
these are the marltarra
the eucalypts with the stringy bark
their name carried from kaurna language
a sound of place older than the vines
older than the fences
or the hands that built them

cloud finds a patch of shade and settles
her fur rising and falling
with the quiet rhythm of trust

claire sets down the thermos and two mugs
pours the tea dark and fragrant
the steam curling through the filtered light
she passes one to fleur
their fingers touch
neither pulls away

for a while they listen
to the slow sigh of wind through leaves
the far off murmur of bees in blossom

softly claire speaks
her voice a resting place
fleur feels her shoulders sink
the air loosen
as the land begins to tell its own slow story

brown stringybark
stands like a grandmother
arms wide
remembering the wind from the south
this is her northern edge claire whispers
beyond this ridge she will not go
fleur observes
the blue gums listen
steady and sure

beneath them golden wattle
burns bright with hope
its pollen the sun made solid
the sheoak bends with quiet song
the wind catching in her fine green hair
and yacca spears rise like candles
their flowers humming with pollinators

down by the creek the world changes its tune
river red gum deep roots drinking old water
silver banksia holding the middle ground
their cones cradling tiny futures
and the manna gum rough and kind
sheds its skin to renew itself

where the shrubs take hold
the wallowa and wirilda
nod like aunties chatting
tea tree and prickly violet
form soft boundaries for the happy wanderers
their branches home for small night singers

by the sedges claire's hands draw maps in air
lepidosperma isolepis cyperus
claire names them like kin
each one a line of belonging
the rushes stitching the creek to the paddock
where moss beds gleam and sundews wait
with glistening patience on the rocks

here too claire says *are the grasses*
the native ones dying under rabbit teeth
and the brazen newcomers
salvation jane bold and greedy
we work to balance them again
to let the ancient soil breathe
the old seeds awake

fleur hears claire's voice slow to a murmur
the science not cold but tender
this is how we mend claire says
parcel by parcel
letting the wild thread itself
back through the rows of vines
until the land remembers
how to breathe whole again

then fleur speaks
her voice soft but certain
i thought i would never come back
i ran when the world closed in
when my parents fell ill
i thought if i moved fast enough
grief would not find me

fleur looks down at the cup in her hands
the surface trembling with her breath
but it found me everywhere
even in sleep
even in air

claire watches her
the sunlight slipping across her face
claire says quietly
grief always finds its way
but so does love
so does healing
sometimes through soil
sometimes through hands

fleur's eyes fill
but she smiles
you sound like the valley itself speaking
claire laughs softly
maybe it's just the tea

cloud stirs
her nose following a beetle through the grass
the moment eases
a kookaburra calls from the fence line
its laughter rolling wide across the paddocks

they sit together in the stillness
tea cooling in their cups
and something unseen begins to root
a fragile beginning
beneath the marltarra gums

chapter eleven the shape of the vine

autumn light folds gold across the hills
the air warm with promise
claire lifts a pair of secateurs
the metal catching the sun
she turns to fleur
you said you wanted to see the real work
not just words and wine

fleur smiles a little shy
i wrote about harvests and terroir fleur says
but always from the table
never the soil
my hands were made for pens not tools
perhaps it is time they learned again

claire nods
then watch first
claire bends to the vine
her body sure and easy
these old trunks
they remember fire and flood
each scar tells you where to cut
you look for new growth
strong enough to hold fruit
not so wild it forgets its roots

fleur kneels beside her
studies the vine's twists
her fingers tracing bark rough and cool
fleur breathes in sap and earth
the faint sweetness
something inside her loosens

fleur tries the secateurs
awkward at first then steady
the clean snip
crisp in the quiet air
a rhythm building between them
cut lift release

claire glances over
you have good hands
fleur laughs softly
they are learning honesty again

cloud drifts through the rows
a grey ghost trailing dust and sunlight
her ears pricked
to the music of secateurs and breath

the work slows as the shadows lengthen
fleur wipes her brow with the back of her wrist
so this is what it means to tend fleur says
to guide but not to own
claire meets her eyes
yes she whispers
to listen more than you take

for a moment they stand still
the vines around them whispering
a chorus of leaves and memory
the valley wide and waiting

and in that hush
their shared silence feels like prayer

evening drifts across marltarra
soft light pouring between the rows
their work done
their bodies slowed
hands stained with good earth
hearts quieter than the morning

cloud trots ahead
her tail a metronome of content
the vineyard hums low with settling birds
an owlet nightjar calls from afar
the first stars begin trembling in the sky

they walk the long track toward the homestead
their silence easy now
the scent of cut vines
sap clinging to them both
fleur brushes soil from her palms
smiles that tired true smile
this day has been a gift fleur says
i had forgotten how the land forgives

claire nods her breath deep and sure
you listen well
it listens back

they reach the gate
and claire pauses
the cottage lights faint beyond the gums
one kilometre of gravel
from here to solitude

claire speaks quietly
almost uncertain
you know fleur
the main house is busy and loud
mike and sue have their rhythm
i have mine over at the cottage
there's space there if you would rather
space to write
to rest
to breathe again

fleur turns her face toward her
surprise softening
into something like relief
are you sure fleur asks
claire smiles small and steady
i am

they keep walking
the path pale under the rising moon
cloud trots beside them
the night fills with the sound of cicadas
and the quiet beginning of something new

chapter thirteen morning in the cottage

the day wakes slow and golden
mist lying low over the paddocks
dew jewelled on the wire fence
the air rich
with the scent of damp earth and eucalyptus

fleur stirs beneath the light quilt
for a moment she forgets where she is
then hears the faint bark of cloud
the sound of claire's boots on gravel outside
and remembers

the cottage breathes around her
walls of timber lined with memory
a kettle sighing on the stove
the old desk by the window
her notebook waiting open
patient

fleur pours coffee dark and steady
sits where light spills across the page
lets her pen move
the words at first halting
then gathering pace
each one tasting of soil and sky
of loss and return
of marltarra

outside
claire is checking the level
of the rain water tank
cloud padding at her heels
claire's voice drifts in with the breeze
a language of rhythm and care
work begins again
but gentler now

fleur watches through the window
her chest full of something she does not name
a quiet joy
shaped like gratitude

fleur writes
the valley is teaching me
how to belong again
how to hold the earth without breaking it
how to listen

a kookaburra
laughs from the fence line
the sound spilling bright into the morning
fleur smiles
the page filling with promise

chapter fourteen breakfast words

claire steps through the open door
boots dusted with earth
the scent of morning
clinging to her skin
she pauses at the sight of fleur
bent over the page
pen moving sure and slow
the light haloing her hair
the steam of the coffee
curling upward
like a quiet prayer

you're up early claire says
fleur looks up smiling
the words would not wait
fleur answers
they have been sleeping too long

claire sets a basket on the table
bread still warm from sue's oven
fresh eggs
a handful of herbs
the small offerings of a shared morning
claire pours coffee and sits opposite
their knees almost touching beneath the table

so what are you writing
claire's voice low gentle curiosity
fleur shrugs
perhaps nothing perhaps everything
just pieces of what i have carried
grief has many shapes
and sometimes it becomes words
sometimes it becomes silence

claire nods slowly
my silence lives in the soil claire says
every planting
every cut
a way to say what i cannot say aloud

fleur reaches across the table
her fingers light against claire's wrist
then how lucky for the valley fleur whispers
that you are still speaking

the touch lingers
neither pulls away
cloud sighs from the doorway
stretching into the sunlight

the moment breathes between them
fragile yet certain
as if the land itself is listening
as if the marltarra
have bent their tall heads
to hear the beginning sounds of love

chapter fifteen ngani the gathering place

morning stretches wide and bright
the vines glistening after light rain
inside the cottage cloud's bath begins
the old enamel tub filled halfway
warm water swirling
with the scent of lavender soap

claire kneels beside her faithful companion
hands steady kind and sure
come on my girl claire murmurs
we are off to ngani today
to visit our elderly friends
you must look your best

cloud steps in with quiet dignity
her coat thick and silver grey
the water turning silky around her
claire rinses
massages
rinses again
talking all the while in that soft working voice
the one she uses for vines and hearts

fleur watches from the doorway
smiling at the ritual
the way care becomes love in motion

after the bath comes the towel
the blow dryer's hum
claire's fingers combing through long fur
the air warm and gentle
little clouds of hair drifting like soft smoke
nails trimmed with careful patience
ready for old hands that bruise easily
because paper thin skin still longs to touch

cloud stands still
tail wagging slow
as if she knows the meaning of this work
she carries peace where ever she goes

when she is done she shines
her coat like morning light on silver bark
she looks up at claire
expectantly
claire laughs
you are beautiful enough to meet everyone
and the elders will do just fine

they load the car
dog lead
blanket
basket of biscuits
fleur climbs in beside them
what is this ngani fleur asks claire

it means gathering place in kaurna language
a place where stories meet
old people live there
where cloud is known and loved

the road winds through the valley
past vines and wildflowers
past history and hope
fleur feels the stillness settle in her chest
watching claire's hands on the wheel
strong
capable
gentle as water

ahead
the small blue signpost
ngani aged care
the morning hums with purpose
as if all the valley breathes with them

chapter sixteen inside ngani

the sign at the entrance reads
ngani
a kaurna word
the gathering place
ngani
a name the air holds gently
as claire parks beneath the blue gums
smooth
mottled
creamy grey bark
like stories retold in time

inside the air is warm
with laughter and floor polish
the clink of teacups
drifting from the kitchen
adjacent to the activity centre
fleur follows claire down the long hallway
her steps hushed by carpet
the colour of autumn leaves
cloud trots beside them
tail slow
head proud
as if she knows her duty

they pass open doors
faces turning to greet them
eyes brightening
hands lifting in recognition
there is our girl someone calls
claire smiles
morning everyone claire says
cloud has come for her cuddles

fleur lingers a step behind
watching as cloud moves
from chair to chair
nosing soft palms
resting her head on thin knees
each touch a small miracle
fleur sees the way the residents soften
how their voices rise like birds
startled into joy
fleur feels tears prick her eyes

claire kneels beside one woman
fixes a loose button with deft fingers
asks after her son
about the last of the tomatoes in the courtyard
her voice full of listening
the woman laughs and says
you always remember

fleur feels something inside her shift
this is not charity fleur thinks
this is community
this is how healing looks
when it walks quietly on four paws

when their round is done
they sit beneath the mural in the sunroom
a painting of vines and river and sky
one old man asks if cloud can stay forever
claire laughs softly
she belongs to the valley she says
but she will always return

fleur writes those words in her mind
knowing they belong to more than the dog

outside the day is warm and bright
when they step into the sunlight again
fleur looks at claire
sees the calm strength in her eyes
understands
love can be built of small acts repeated
like pruning
like watering
like showing up again and again

the road winds gentle
through the valley
afternoon light slipping between the trees
the air still sweet
the scent of hand lotion and tea
the soft mixture of humanity and hope

cloud sleeps in the back seat
head resting on her paws
a small sigh of contentment
her work done

fleur sits in the passenger seat
notebook open on her knees
words forming in slow steady lines
not about grief this time
but about grace
about hands that mend
the power of touch
that asks for nothing in return

claire drives in silence
one hand on the wheel
one arm brown from sun
her gaze steady on the road ahead
the window open
to the soft smell of autumn vines
and gum leaves
the faint call of magpies drifting through

fleur glances at her
feels the warmth that hums between them
not the sudden fire of memory
but something deeper
quieter
the slow burning kind that endures

ngani fleur says softly
the gathering place
it felt like time stood still there
claire nods
it is a good place
it reminds me that even in endings
there can be beginnings

fleur closes her notebook
rests her head against the seat
the valley rolls out before them
shades of green and gold
endlessly forgiving
she thinks of how she will write this
how she will tell of cloud and claire
the people of *ngani*
how she will let the land speak through her again

as they turn down the track to marltarra
cloud lifts her head
tail thumping
and claire smiles
home claire says simply
and the word feels vast
fleur feels it settle in her bones
like a promise

evening settles soft upon marltarra
a hush between the vines
the air cool now
sweet with crushed mint and soil
the last birds threading home across the sky

fleur sits by the open window
the small lamp pooling gold across her page
her notebook open
her pen moving steady
writing the story of *ngani*
of laughter and touch
of old hands
the calm grey dog
of gathering
not in sorrow
but in grace

her words flow easier than before
the sentences uncoiling like vines finding light
she writes of claire too
not by name
not yet
but as a woman of soil and silence
whose kindness ripples outward
like water released from a well

outside on the verandah
claire moves in rhythm
sweeping the dust from the boards
checking tools
laying them neat in their crate
the kind of order that steadies her heart
cloud sprawled beside her
paws twitching in sleep
the scent of soap still clinging to her fur

fleur pauses lifts her head
watches the shape of claire in twilight
her outline sure
her gestures simple
each one full of quiet grace
fleur feels the pull again
not sharp now
but deep like the tide

fleur writes
healing begins in the hands that stay
in the voices that listen
in the breath shared
between silence and trust

the light fades
frogs start their chorus by the dam
the world folding into peace

claire steps inside
wipes her hands on a cloth
you are still writing she says
fleur smiles
i am finding my way back
through words

good claire answers
and sets the kettle on the stove

for a while they move around each other
easy unhurried
the kind of companionship
that asks for nothing
and offers everything

outside the marltarra stand tall
their stringy bark
whispering
in the cool night breeze
inside the cottage
two women work quietly toward morning
one shaping words
the other shaping life

night drifts close around the cottage
the marltarra hum with wind
the lamp throws a circle of warm gold
fleur's notebook lies open
ink still drying on the last page

claire pours the tea
sets the mugs between them
cloud shifts beside the hearth
her fur rising and falling
in the quiet rhythm of sleep

for a while they listen
to the frogs
the crackle of small flames
the peace of the valley
holding them both steady

then claire says
you wrote deep tonight
it is there in your eyes
what were you seeing

fleur breathes slow
her voice low as memory
i was seeing
the hospital corridors
the masks
the sound of ventilators
the emptiness that came after
how i stopped speaking
because every word felt too fragile

fleur looks at cloud
curled
dreaming
it was different today fleur says
with cloud there
so calm
so patient
people forgot their fear for a while
i forgot mine

her hand moves gently
tracing the rim of the cup
this place
you and cloud
you made it possible for me
to remember without drowning
to say what happened
not to break

claire reaches across
rests her hand lightly on fleur's
no need to hurry claire says
the land teaches us that
healing takes seasons
not days

fleur nods
tears quiet on her cheeks
she smiles
it feels like breathing again fleur whispers
for the first time in so long

cloud stirs in her sleep
gives a soft sigh
as if she understands

outside the earth breathes with the night
under the marltarra
the air is full of grace

the spring dawn slips softly
through mist and gum
dew clings to every blade of grass
the valley smells of eucalyptus
fresh beginning
cloud stretches
yawns
shakes the sleep from her coat
waits at the door
tail slow with expectation

claire ties her boots
pulls on her faded hat
today claire says *we are off to the bushgardens*
there is work to do and friends to see
fleur looks up from her cup
bushgardens she asks uncertainly
yes claire smiles
a place where plants and people heal together

they drive the winding road
through waking light
paddocks shining with the first sun
magpies calling from fence posts
the kind of morning that forgives everything

at the gate the sign reads
bushgardens
native revegetation
community renewal
the words painted by many hands

inside the fence the air hums
young wattles trembling gold
eremophilas bright with bloom
soil rich
dark underfoot
volunteers working
their voices low and kind

claire moves among them easily
checking seedlings
noting growth
her voice sure and gentle
fleur follows watching
seeing how every gesture speaks
belonging

this is my heart place claire says
we plant not just for beauty
but for balance
for the land to breathe again
fleur bends to touch the soil
it smells alive fleur whispers

fleur helps lift trays of seedlings
tiny roots twirled in damp soil
claire shows her where to dig
how to loosen the earth without tearing
how to plant firm but kind
this is caring claire says
this is partnership with country
not command

cloud trots between them
her fur bright against the brown path
ears twitching
to the sounds of tools and birds
not resentful of the rules
dogs on leads

fleur looks around at the circle of workers
different ages
different stories
hands dirty
faces shining
and she feels the same slow opening
that began at *ngani*

the valley fleur thinks
is teaching me to belong again

the big shed is open to the morning
cups of tea steaming in the hands of attendees
slides flickering across the white wall
light and soil alive in close-up dance

claire stands easy before them
her voice calm as soft rain on dry ground
this is where it begins claire says
invisible worlds beneath our feet

claire shows the web of hyphae
delicate threads of fungi
linking root to root
sharing sugars and song
feeding the grasses and gums alike

fleur watches the colours shift
under the microscope camera
a shimmer of gold and blue filaments
a hidden city of exchange and trust
life talking to life
in languages unseen

claire speaks of the harm done
by compaction
by chemical haste
by grazing too long in one place
the silence that follows
when the mycelium fall away

then claire speaks of return
how mulch
rest and patience
awaken the sleeping networks
how compost and native cover
are acts of healing
not labour

claire gestures to the screen again
a living lace glowing with promise
diversity claire says *is resilience*
the soil remembers kindness
if only we give it breath and time

fleur feels her pulse steady
the rhythm of curiosity and trust
as claire speaks the language of soil
not softly now
but with certainty
her laboratory becomes a window
into the living world beneath their feet
slides glowing with threads of fungi
notes alive with data and devotion
this is the science fleur had longed to find
where care and beauty share the same breath
the land begins to breathe again

the sun now stands high above the valley
its light spilling white across the soil
inside the big shed the air is cool
smelling of soil and eucalyptus oil
like something good baking

fleur pauses before the noticeboard
a flyer bright with ochre and sky
words of co-design and kinship
first nations wisdom
shaping care for country
the landscape board
listening learning walking beside
volunteers with hands in soil
hearts open
fleur feels hope take gentle root

volunteers gather
in the long shadow of the doorway
their laughter rising easy
between bites of fresh bread
cheese and olives
flasks open
the hiss of thermos lids
the creak of benches
the rustle of waxed paper
unwrapping sandwiches

claire passes a plate of sue's scones
warmed from the shed's microwave oven
butter melting in gold rivulets
try one claire says to fleur
they taste of home

fleur smiles
her fingers sticky with quandong jam
the fruit of the *santalum acuminatum*
shared from the volunteers in the arid zone

fleur listens to the talk that rolls around her
stories of planting days and seed drives
of floods and how the reeds came back
of echidnas seen again
by the creek
each voice threaded with care
with memory
with pride

fleur feels something shift inside
a loosening
a deep slow breath
she had not known she was holding

around her
these people speak as if the land is family
as if every shrub is a cousin
every bird a returning friend
their sentences full of we and us
never i nor mine

fleur looks across at claire
hair caught in the soft light
eyes alive with quiet purpose
fleur understands
this is what healing looks like
not silence
but the murmur of belonging

fleur feels the ache of her own edges
how grief still lives there tender raw
but also the beginning of mending
the knowledge that to help others
she must first learn to hold herself whole

cloud dozes beneath the table
tail tapping the rhythm of life
a child reaches down to pat her
cloud sighs her small sound of peace

outside the wind moves through the trees
the sheoaks whisper to the wattles
fleur knows she is listening now
with more than her ears

chapter twenty two the evening

dusk folds soft around marltarra
the air inside warm with woodsmoke
the faint perfume of herbs
crickets begin their song in the grass
the first stars tremble above the ridge

inside the cottage the lamp hums low
fleur sits at the table
notebook open
her fingers inked
her thoughts spilling free
fleur writes of the shed
the people
of laughter shared with strangers

the sound of soil
when it yields to planting hands
of a land that invites mending
of how her own heart
has begun to listen

outside claire rinses the tools
hangs gloves to dry beneath the verandah
the quiet pride of honest work
still in her shoulders

cloud lies nearby
muzzle on paws
half asleep
half dreaming of the day's kindness

claire steps inside
wiping her hands on a cloth
sees fleur bent over the page
the look of peace rare and new across her face
you are writing again claire says softly
fleur responds without looking up
about them
about us
about the way this valley teaches

claire moves closer
reads the words upside down
smiles at the line that says
healing is a language
spoken by the land
by those who care for it

claire pours two cups of tea
sets one by fleur's hand
then sits across from her
the kind of silence that needs no filling
the one made of understanding

after a while fleur closes the notebook
her eyes shining in the lamplight
it feels different now fleur says
the words don't hurt
they grow

claire reaches
to tuck a loose curl behind fleur's ear
then leaves her hand there
a heartbeat longer than habit
i'm glad claire whispers
we all need to grow again sometime

cloud shifts
stretches
sighs
the night deepens around them
the valley breathing slow and sure
as if it too eavesdrops on their quiet becoming

sunlight spills through the cottage window
the day already stretching bright across the hills
the smell of toast and eucalyptus
drifts between the rooms
cloud thumps her tail in greeting
as mike's ute crunches on the gravel drive

sue hops out first
all laughter and wind-tossed hair
a basket in her arms
you two hiding away again sue teases
i have fresh scones and gossip to share

fleur smiles from the doorway
the warmth of sue's tone
a balm
it feels good to be found in such light

they sit at the table
mugs steaming
bread breaking
sue's voice a bright river of plans
there's a festival coming sue says
music
markets
bush tucker stalls
and we're hoping for a display
from the bushgardens
stories of land care
and renewal
you should come along fleur
maybe help tell our story

fleur listens
her heart lifting
the old impulse stirring
to write for others
to give voice to place and people
but beneath it
lies a quieter truth
that she is not quite ready
her soil needs tending first

fleur smiles gently
thank you fleur says
it sounds wonderful
i think i will need a little longer
to learn my own story again
before i tell anyone else's

sue nods easily
unfazed
of course sue says
no rush just come
breathe it in
be part of it

claire meets fleur's eyes across the table
a look of knowing between them
the kind that needs no speech
renewal takes time it says
the valley has patience

they sit a while longer
the talk rolling soft as wind in the vines
when the ute finally drives away
fleur steps outside
the morning wide before her
alive with promise and quiet resolve

fleur breathes deep
feeling her roots sink in
just a little deeper
into this place
it is mending her

chapter twenty four walking and wondering

the sun leans warm across the vines
air thick with the hum of bees
and promise
fleur walks alone
notebook in hand
her boots brushing the soft soil of the track
cloud trails behind
nose to the wind
faithful as a shadow

fleur writes as she walks
small lines scattered like seed
belonging fleur writes
is not ownership
it is the slow weaving of breath with place

fleur pauses to rest against a post
the valley rolling wide before her
new grape leaves
flashing silver in the breeze
in her chest
a tug of wanting
for home
for rest
for claire

fleur smiles at herself wry and tender
what does a lesbian bring on a second date
her furniture
the old joke
circling in her mind

a reminder to keep space around her heart
to let love breathe
not to fold her whole self
into another's life
no matter how kind the waiting arms

fleur thinks of alsace
the long corridors of hospitals
the lockdowns
the lockouts
the echo of sirens
the muffled goodbyes
the apartment that grew smaller each month
the way silence became a second skin
fleur knows the danger of mistaking safety
for salvation
knows she must stand steady
before she leans

fleur writes
i am not here to be rescued
i am here to recover
to rebuild from the inside out
to learn how to stay

cloud circles back
nudges fleur's knee
eyes bright
tail slow
as if to say *you are doing fine*
step by step

fleur closes her notebook
looks toward the cottage roof
glinting through the trees
feels the valley breathe with her
soft patient forgiving
a place that asks for truth
before devotion

fleur turns homeward
the scent of crushed leaves rising around her
each breath a promise
she will come to love
without losing herself again

night folds around the cottage
a stillness broken only by the sigh of wind
through marltarra
the soft hiss of the fire in the hearth
cloud stretched long before the flames
her fur flickering silver in the light

claire pours tea into heavy mugs
sets them on the table
the scent of peppermint rising with the steam
she watches fleur's hands resting on her journal
the ink smudged from use
a map of heart and healing

fleur's voice comes quiet
measured
like someone
crossing a river of ghosts
in alsace it was different fleur begins
the sirens never stopped
every night another street closed
another friend gone
the air thick with disinfectant
fear
the hospital windows were sealed shut
i opened them in my mind
imagined the valley here
the light
the vines
the scent of dust and eucalyptus
but even my dreams grew tired
my mother died alone
my father followed slowly
and i stopped believing in breath

her hands tremble
fleur keeps speaking
i thought the world had ended
then i came here
and you gave me work
tea and quiet
a dog who carries peace in her fur
the land
oh claire
this land is sanctuary
it asks nothing
offers everything
teaching me to live again

claire listens
her eyes deep as evening sky
when she finally speaks
her voice is soft

when our parents died
marltarra came to mike and me
neither of us ready for the weight of that gift
our parents' hands had planted this place
in the nineteen seventies
to save the remnant marltarra gums
their life's work
a quiet devotion
balancing conservation with the need to live
rows of vines
stitched carefully beside old trees
viticulture that grew slowly
into something wiser
sustainable soil deep with meaning

from them i learned to listen to the earth's breath
to see the life beneath my feet
so the soil laboratory came to be
a way of continuing their vow
their death changed everything
but the roots they tended
still hold us steady

claire continued
after my parents died i was like you
i buried myself in work
mending vines fixing fences
telling myself the earth needed me
but really i needed the earth
its rhythm kept me breathing
it reminded me
that loss and life share the same soil

fleur nods
tears shining unashamed
we are alike then fleur says
both learning to grow again

they sit in the hush
the fire crackling like memory releasing
outside
frogs *pobblebonk*
continuously from the dam
the valley seems to lean closer
to listen to two women
finding their way home

claire reaches out
not to comfort but to share stillness
her fingers brush fleur's
and stay

cloud sighs a long contented sound
the marltarra murmur in the wind
the night folds around them
warm
wide
forgiving

dawn breathes pale gold through the curtains
the light spilling across the quilt
fleur lies still for a long moment
listening to the soft sounds of the cottage
the kettle beginning to hum
cloud's tail
brushing faintly against the floorboards

outside the vines glow with morning dew
birds tracing the air with song
fleur feels that fragile thing inside her
the one she thought was gone
beginning to flutter again

fleur rises
wraps herself in a shawl
steps barefoot onto the verandah
the wood cool beneath her feet
the world wide
forgiving

in her pocket her passport rests
creased from travel and grief
a reminder that she is here
but not of here
a visitor

a guest in this generous land
on kaurna country
fleur whispers the truth of it
to the marltarra trees
standing tall beyond the fence
i will not take what is not mine
i will listen
i will learn

fleur thinks of claire
already down by the vines
the morning light finding her shoulders
strong and sure against the rows of green
fleur's heart fills with a quiet ache
love and gratitude tangled together

fleur knows she cannot stay forever
the visa stamped with time's small boundary
but she also knows
that healing does not ask for permanence
only presence

fleur opens her notebook
and writes
sanctuary is not escape
it is the place where courage returns

fleur looks out across marltarra
the valley opening like a promise
breathes deep
she will keep writing
keep walking
keep finding the balance
between holding on and letting go

behind her cloud pads softly
leans against her leg
as if to say
you belong for now
and that is enough

the morning is cool
clear light spills through the vines
smell of toast drifting from the cottage
claire stands at the stove
her hair still damp from the shower
cloud curled at her feet
the image of small domestic peace

fleur comes in softly
notebook in hand
her eyes bright yet shadowed
fleur smiles
a little tentative
claire hands her a mug of coffee
their fingers brush a familiar warmth
no words needed at first
the comfort of shared silence

then claire says
you were up early again
fleur nods
i was writing
trying to untangle this feeling
of loving a place
while knowing i cannot stay

claire looks at her
steady kind
the way she looks at vines she cannot control
but tends anyway
you're talking about your visa claire says quietly

fleur sighs
yes
a visitor only
such a small word
for such a large truth
i don't know what comes next
if i leave i lose this
you
the land
this peace
yet if i try to hold it too tight
it will slip away

claire stirs the porridge slowly
the rhythm of thought in her spoon
claire says
the land has taught me
that everything is temporary
the seasons turn
the vines rest
even grief changes its shape
what matterss
is how we love in the time we have

fleur listens
her throat tight with the beauty of these words
fleur sets her notebook on the table
in it the words she wrote just after dawn
sanctuary is not escape
it is the place where courage returns

fleur reads them aloud
and claire nods
then maybe this place
has already done what it needed to do
you are brave again
you are here

fleur smiles
half sorrow half light
perhaps
but still i wish for more

claire steps close
brushes the hair from fleur's eyes
more will come
in its own season

cloud lifts her head
tail sweeping the floor
as if agreeing
with the wisdom of the moment

they sit together to eat
the valley waking beyond the window
magpies singing the new day into being
in the gentle rhythm of their shared breath
both women know
love need not be forever
to be true

chapter twenty eight walking the boundary

late afternoon light slants across the vines
each row a green chorus to patience
western grey kangaroos
drift slowly between them
unhurried
while cloud's ears flick
her tail brushing soil into sunbeams
kangaroo shapes parting the air
like soft thoughts

claire and fleur walk side by side
hands brushing but not holding
their words small in the wide stillness
above them cockatoos wheel white against blue
their cries sharp and joyful
magpies answering in deeper tones
the sound of country talking to itself

the ground beneath them
soft with wallaby grass
tufts silver and fine
seed heads trembling in the breeze
between their feet tiny yellow buttons bloom
their faces small suns
smiling from the earth

they pause where the fence meets the creek line
a sleepy lizard basks on the warm gravel
unhurried
ancient
his blue tongue flicking out a greeting

fleur laughs softly
he reminds me of an old alsaceian poet
wise
slow
full of secrets
claire grins
and just as stubborn

they stand watching the vines breathe
listening to the hum of bees
to the pulse of water hidden deep in the soil
fleur says quietly
this place will stay in me
even when i go
like a rhythm learned by heart

claire nods
that is what the land does
it teaches you how to return
even if you never come back

fleur looks out across marltarra
the rows fading into the distance
each post a marker of time and care
fleur feels both sadness and peace
the ache of endings
softened by gratitude

cloud trots ahead
her fur bright against the green
a small faithful presence
leading them home

the cockatoos rise again
their wings flashing white in the sun
for a moment
everything holds still
the vines
the wind
the two women
bound not by promise
but by understanding

they turn back along the boundary
the sky wide above them
their steps slow
deliberate
each one a quiet vow
to carry the valley within

night folds down over marltarra
the sky a slow river of stars
the scent of rain drifting from the ranges
frogs singing from the dam
their rhythm the heart of the valley

fleur sits at the old table
lamp light pooling around her page
the window open to the cool breeze
cloud asleep by the hearth
claire somewhere outside
checking water tank levels
beneath the marltarra gums

fleur's pen moves slowly
deliberate
each word a breath of letting go
fleur writes
i came here as a visitor
my passport heavy with endings
my heart unanchored
i found soil that listened
hands that healed without words
a dog who carried calm benediction
a woman who taught me
that tending the earth
is another form of desire

fleur pauses
listens to the night
the call of a mopoke settling in
the faint chatter of cockatoos finding roost
the murmur of leaves like water over stone

fleur writes again
this valley does not promise forever
it promises presence
to live here even briefly
is to learn how to breathe again

her eyes blur with quiet tears
not of sorrow but of gratitude
the kind that comes when pain and peace
finally sit side by side

fleur closes the notebook
lays her hand upon its cover
feeling the pulse of words still warm within
and whispers
merci

claire steps in softly
wiping dust from her hands
you have been writing again
fleur nods
yes
something that feels like goodbye
and like beginning

claire smiles
both can be true

outside the marltarra sway in the wind
their stringy bark whispering the oldest lullaby
inside two women sit together
in the glow of small light
each knowing
that some love belongs
not to possession
but to simple grace
having found each other after all

chapter thirty the leaving

first light brushes the vines silver
dew trembling on each leaf
the air cool full of promise and ache
cloud trots ahead
nose to the ground
ears flicking at the sound of waking birds

fleur walks beside claire
their steps slow
deliberate
boots pressing memory into the soil
the valley still half asleep
crows calling from the ridge
magpies stitching song into the sky

they say little
words seem too small
for what lives between them
the air itself carrying what they mean
gratitude
affection
the ache of leaving
fleur reaches down
lets her fingers graze the tops of wallaby grass
feels the softness
life still moving beneath dew

this place fleur whispers
it has changed me
it taught me to breathe again
claire nods her eyes steady on the horizon
that is what it does
you give to it and it gives back
in its own time
in its own way

they stop
where the rows open to the creek
the water thin but singing
fleur kneels
touches the surface
cold
clear
alive
i will miss this fleur says
claire smiles
it will wait for you
the land keeps its stories

cloud circles back
leans against fleur's leg
tail slow
gentle
as if to offer comfort
or blessing

fleur straightens
turns to claire
their faces close in the morning light
thank you fleur says
for everything
for not asking me to be more
than i could be

claire shakes her head
you already are more
just by being here

the sun edges higher
burning mist from the paddocks
the flora glowing green gold
alive
fleur breathes deep
the scent of earth and eucalyptus fill her
she will carry it home
carry it always

they walk back toward the cottage
cloud bounding ahead
the gravel crunching
softly beneath their feet
though neither speaks
both know this is not an ending
only the gentle turning of another season

chapter forty letters

weeks pass
then months
seasons turn their quiet wheel
the vines at marltarra
heavy with fruit again
on claire's kitchen table
a letter rests among the laboratory papers

postmarked france
the envelope pale green
edges smudged from travel
her name written in looping script
claire collins marltarra
southern barossa valley
a small flower image taped on the back
yellow button flower
tiny and bright

claire opens it
slowly
the paper smelling faintly of rosemary
and ink
each line drawn in fleur's steady hand
the words lean slightly
as if eager to speak

dear claire
it begins
the valley still lives in me
each morning when i walk through alsace rain
i hear the magpies
i see wallaby grass
in the shimmer of city parks

your hands
your laughter
the soft sound of cloud's paws on the deck
all live quietly beneath my breath

i am writing again on real paper
no screens
no glow
only pen and heartbeat
because some truths deserve to travel slowly
i have finished my piece
about marltarra and ngani and the bushgardens
it will be printed next month
i wanted to send you these words
first
the ones that matter most

you taught me
that tending is another name for love
that healing grows in circles
not in straight lines
that home is not a fixed place
but the pulse of belonging
found in kindness

at the bottom of the page
small illustrations bloom
wallaby grass swaying gentle
yellow buttons on sage green stalks
each drawn with the care of gratitude

beneath them fleur's final words
until the seasons and you
call me south again
know that the land and i
are both learning to breathe

fais de beaux rêves
have sweet dreams

claire folds the letter
lays her hand upon it
feels its warmth
travelling up through her chest
outside the marltarra whisper
white cockatoos wheel across the pale blue sky
cloud lifts her head
as if hearing a familiar voice on the wind

writing

i wrote of marltarra
because the land itself is a teacher
a quiet voice beneath the wind
that asks us to see what endures
to walk gently within this living web
to remember that sustainability is not a choice
but a way of being in relationship

on marltarra soil the old roots breathe again
beneath the brown stringybark *eucalyptus baxteri*
the northernmost stand in south australia
its many trunks shaped by the axes once used
to feed the nuriootpa brick kilns long ago
now growing freely
reclaiming their form

blue gums *eucalyptus leucoxylon*
river red gums *eucalyptus camaldulensis*
stretch wide across the gullies
their branches sheltering
native pine *callitris gracilis*
and drooping sheoak *allocasuarina verticillata*
their fallen needles soft underfoot
holding moisture in the summer heat

beneath them yaccas *xanthorrhoea semiplana*
spread their skirts beside golden wattles
acacia pycnantha
and tea trees *leptospermum continentale*
silver banksias *banksia marginata* feed the birds
while lavender grevillea *grevillea lavandulacea*
fringe myrtle *calytrix tetragona*
light the spring with colour

among the granite outcrops hide
the green-flowered hairy correa *correa aemula*
and the rare prickly tree violet *melicytus dentatus*
offering safe homes to thornbills and wrens
proof that even fragile things endure
when given space and care

mistletoe *amyema miquelii*
threads through eucalypt and acacia
feeding new holland honeyeater
phylidonyris novaehollandiae
and mistletoe bird
dicaeum hirundinaceum
while lichens paint the stone with patience
turning rock to soil over centuries

kangaroos *macropus fuliginosus* graze the clearings
sleepy lizards *tiliqua rugosa* bask in the warmth
superb fairy-wrens *malurus cyaneus*
flash their blue in the reeds
and kookaburras *dacelo novaeguineae*
call laughter through the trees at dawn

this is marltarra
not just a place
but a promise
that land can heal when hands listen
that sustainability begins in understanding
that every story written here
is an offering of gratitude
to the earth that sustains us all

marltarra means stringy bark gum
a kaurna word for the trees
standing watch over the valley
their bark rough and beautiful
their roots deep in story
this land of southern barossa
has always been a place of gathering
of seed and song and shared labour

these verses were written in respect
for country
for all first peoples
whose care of land continues beyond measure
their knowledge shaping our understanding
of how to live gently
how to listen
before we act

to the community of the valley
to those who plant
who prune
who pour
who volunteer
visit and keep the stories alive
these pages belong also to you

to the women who love women
who find themselves remade
by kindness and soil
by dogs who carry calm in their fur
may you know that belonging is not given
it is grown

to the reader
thank you for walking these vineyard rows
for hearing the magpies
the cockatoos
the frogs
for feeling the dust
the dew
the breath of marltarra
may you leave these words
with earth under your nails
and renewal in your heart

Deb. Always willing to read my words. Always supportive of
LGBTQIA+.
Always ready for an adventure.
And didn't ridicule me when I used *and* at least a thousand
times in this small document. At the beginning of almost every
line.
I phoned and complained, 'You are reducing my word count
by crossing out *and* at the beginning of every line. The
document is at least a thousand words less now.'
We laughed. Seriously, though, Deb always approaches reading
my work conscientiously. I sincerely appreciate it.

Karen Marree. Always patient. Always kind. Always willing to try
a new approach to internal design to get the flow of words out
in the world.

Joy and *Kalika* at Centred in Choice for the inaugural meeting in
Coober Pedy during September 2019. The grand plans, the
shared values, then Covid and the pivot from print to ebooks.
Who knew this is where we would be in 2025?

Cloud, my blue merle Shetland Sheepdog with the official long
name who changed my life and showed me that career changes
are truly possible: from show dog and breeder to accredited
therapy dog at shopping centres and special schools, to calm
kayaker, eager traveller, and photographic model. Calm
companion each time the autoimmune disease flared up and
attempted to smother me. Cloud. The perfect dog.

thanking

Thank you to the authors and contributors to "Kaurna
Warrapiipa"
Kaurna Dictionary
(ISBN 978 1 74305 921 0).

The Kaurna words chosen specifically for this narrative include

marltarra *n* species of gum tree (similar to stringy bark)

ngani *n* gathering place